Kate
the Royal Wedding Fairy

Special thanks to
Rachel Elliot

Wishing Charlotte and James
a magical wedding day

ORCHARD BOOKS
338 Euston Road, London NW1 3BH
Orchard Books Australia
Level 17/207 Kent Street, Sydney, NSW 2000
A Paperback Original

First published in 2011 by Orchard Books

A CIP catalogue record for this book is available
from the British Library.

ISBN 978 1 40831 524 8

5 7 9 10 8 6 4

Printed in Great Britain

The paper and board used in this paperback are natural recyclable
products made from wood grown in sustainable forests. The
manufacturing processes conform to the environmental regulations
of the country of origin.

Orchard Books is a division of Hachette Children's Books,
an Hachette UK company

www.hachette.co.uk

Kate
the Royal Wedding Fairy

by Daisy Meadows

ORCHARD BOOKS

www.rainbowmagic.co.uk

The Fairyland Palace

Chapel

Royal Workshop

Spiral Tower

Crypt

Jack Frosl's
Ice
Castle

Throne
Room

The fairies are planning a royal event,
But I have a scheme that will make them lament!
I'll steal the royal fairy's gold glimmering crown,
And all true love hopes will come tumbling down.

Come goblins, come servants, we'll go in disguise,
And keep out of sight of those bright fairy eyes.
Only someone like me who is handsome and clever,
Can stop happy endings for ever and ever!

Contents

Flower Power!

"Spring is my favourite season," said Rachel Walker, swinging her roller-skates happily.

"And mine," said her best friend Kirsty Tate. "I love seeing all the bright flowers."

Kirsty was spending half term in Tippington with Rachel and they had been roller-skating in the park all morning.

"I wonder what's for lunch," said Kirsty. "All that skating has made me really hungry."

"Me too," said Rachel. Suddenly she stopped and stared at one of the flowerbeds in surprise.

"What's the matter?" asked Kirsty, stopping as well.

"Look at that rose," said Rachel. "There's something odd about it . . ."

All the other flowers were nodding and bowing in the light spring breeze, but one deep-red rose wasn't moving. It was standing up very tall and stiff, like a soldier on parade.

"Its petals are all folded up tightly," exclaimed Kirsty, taking a step towards it.

"And it's glowing!" Rachel added in excitement. "Oh Kirsty, I think something magical is about to happen!"

The girls had been lucky enough to have many adventures in Fairyland, and were great friends with all the Rainbow Magic fairies. They heard a faint tinkling of bells, and then the rose's petals opened slowly, revealing a tiny, beautiful fairy. She had long, shining brown hair topped by a sparkling tiara. She was wearing a stunning gown of ivory silk, and a dazzling gold pendant hung around her neck. On her feet were delicate shoes set with sparkling diamonds.

"Hello," she said in a silvery voice. "I'm Kate the Royal Wedding Fairy."

"It's wonderful to meet you!" Kirsty replied with a big smile.

"I'm so pleased that I found you both," said Kate. "We desperately need your help! Please will you come to Fairyland at once? I will explain everything when we get there."

"Of course we'll come!" said Rachel and Kirsty together. The girls both knew that time would stand still while they were in Fairyland.

Kate gave a relieved smile and waved her wand. Tiny pink roses and red heart

shapes swirled from the wand's tip and
surrounded the girls. Rachel and Kirsty
felt themselves becoming smaller as they
were lifted into the air and placed gently
in the velvety heart of the rose. Looking
over their shoulders, they saw gauzy
wings fluttering on their backs.

Kate waved her wand again, and
the rose's petals began to close and
shimmering golden sparkles spun around
the girls. In no time at all, they were
flying above the glimmering Fairyland
Palace.

"It's so lovely to be back!" said Rachel
as they swooped downwards to the
palace's entrance.

"Look, there's Mia the Bridesmaid
Fairy!" cried Kirsty, spotting their old
friend. "Hello, Mia!"

13

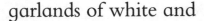

Mia hurried forwards as they landed
and gave them both a big hug.

"It's lovely to see you again," she said.
Behind her, the Petal Fairies were
hard at work decorating the door with
garlands of white and
pink flowers. They
waved to the
girls.

"What's
happening
today?" asked
Rachel.

"There is going to be a
very special wedding here this afternoon,"
Kate explained. "You see, I'm in charge
of making sure that all weddings, but
especially royal weddings, go well in both
Fairyland and the human world."

"Queen Titania has asked you to take the girls to the Seeing Pool, Kate," said Mia. "She'll meet you there."

"Now I must go and help the bridesmaids get ready. I'll see you all later!"

Kate led the girls towards the Seeing Pool in the palace garden.

"I'm so grateful that you have come to help us," she said.

"We're always happy to help," said Kirsty. "But what exactly has happened?"

"Well," said Kate, with a frown. "Jack Frost has put the happiness of a very special royal couple at risk!"

The Goblinovski Festival Ballet

As they fluttered towards the Seeing Pool, Kate explained what had happened.

"King Oberon and Queen Titania's niece, Princess Grace, is getting married this afternoon," she said. "Everyone has been looking forward to this day for weeks. There are celebrations and parties planned all over Fairyland."

"And are all the fairies doing something
to help?" asked Rachel, remembering the
Petal Fairies decorating the palace door.

"Yes, everyone wants to be involved
in the wedding," said Kate with a smile.
"The Party Fairies are organising the
reception. The Music Fairies
have composed a
brand-new piece
of music for the
occasion. The
Dance Fairies
have been
teaching everyone
how to do a special
dance for the day,

and the Rainbow Fairies are creating a
wedding rainbow that will light up the
sky with its beautiful colours."

"That all sounds wonderful!" said Rachel with a happy sigh. "I love weddings, and I expect a royal wedding is really spectacular."

"What is your job, Kate?" Kirsty asked, as they landed beside the glassy Seeing Pool.

"To help me look after royal weddings, I am in charge of the True Love Crown," said Kate. "Its magic is very special, because it creates a bond between the wearer and his or her true love that can never be broken, and it guarantees that they will live happily ever after."

"How lovely!" said Rachel.

"The crown is magnificent," said Kate, "and I always keep it safely locked up in the Spiral Tower, watched over by a legion of frog guards."

"Princess Grace must wear the True Love Crown when she says her marriage vows," Kate continued, "otherwise there's no guarantee that the royal couple will live happily ever after. But yesterday something terrible happened. The True Love Crown was taken from the tower to be polished, because it has been ten years since the last royal wedding. But as the guard was carrying the crown from the tower to the workshop . . ."

Kate's voice trembled slightly, and she paused.

"What happened?" asked Rachel.

"Let me show you," said a familiar, friendly voice behind them.

The girls whirled around and saw Queen Titania standing there. They curtseyed as she walked towards them, holding out her hands.

"Thank you both for coming," she said. "We know that we can always depend on your help."

She waved her wand over the Seeing Pool, and the water whirled and shimmered for a moment. Then a picture appeared, and the girls saw a young frog guard standing beside a spiralling tower of gleaming white marble.

"Look, there's Bertram the footman!" cried Rachel, recognising their old friend.

Bertram was handing the young frog guard a red velvet cushion, on which rested a beautiful golden crown, sparkling with many beautiful jewels.

"Be very careful as you take the True Love Crown to the workshop, Stanley," he said. "Don't let it out of your sight for a moment."

Stanley the frog guard nodded solemnly.

Looking very proud to be given such a big responsibility, he set off towards the palace. But as he walked past the green in front of the Spiral Tower, something caught his eye.

There was a ragged old screen standing on the green nearby, and a troupe of dancers was practising in front of it, their tutus fluttering around them as they leapt and pranced. They were wearing sparkly tights and feathery hair decorations. When they saw Stanley watching, they called out to him.

"Do you like dancing?"

"Come and watch us practise!"

"We're the best dancers in the world!"

"Don't miss out on seeing the famous Goblinovski Festival Ballet!"

Stanley looked down at the True Love Crown.

"But I have to get this to the workshop as fast as I can," he said.

"You'll never get another chance like this," said one of the dancers in a wheedling voice. "It's the opportunity of a lifetime!"

"But . . . but . . ." stammered Stanley.

"A few minutes won't make any difference," interrupted another, who was wearing a grubby purple tutu. "Besides, we need an audience!

 We've been practising our new piece all day to give Princess Grace a big surprise on her wedding day."

Stanley, looking very bewildered, stood and watched as the dance troupe took their positions.

"The Goblinovski Festival Ballet is delighted to present 'A Spring Surprise'," announced the plumpest dancer.

Then someone yelled, "GO!" and they all began to leap about, shouting out explanations in a very confusing way.

"I'm a moth!" yelled one.

"I'm a mosquito!" bellowed another. "Bzzz!"

"I'm a weed!'
"A turkey!"
"A snail!"

It was the strangest dance routine that
Rachel or Kirsty had ever seen, and it
was obvious that Stanley thought so
too. He stood watching with his mouth
hanging open in astonishment. Suddenly
the dancer in the purple tutu bounded up
to him.

"We are very lucky to have a special guest with us today," he announced in ringing tones. "The dancer of dancers, the cream of the crop, the most amazing dancer in the world – Frostyev!"

Goblin Trickery!

A dancer leapt out dressed in a spiky silver tutu and a large feathery head-dress that completely covered his face. The girls watched in astonishment as Frostyev danced crazily across the green. Stanley's eyes were almost popping out of his head. The green was alive with cavorting dancers and loud squawks as they crashed into each other.

Finally, after one last mad whirl,
Frostyev and the dancers finished and
looked expectantly at Stanley. Politely, he
placed the cushion on the ground in front
of him and clapped loudly. But when
he finished clapping and looked down,
he gave a cry of horror. Instead of the
True Love Crown, a large

cabbage was sitting
on the red velvet
cushion!

"Thieves!
Robbers!" cried
Stanley, rushing
towards the ballet
troupe.

Frostyev pulled out a wand and sent
an ice-bolt flying towards him, pulling
off his tutu and head-dress as he did so.

As Stanley ducked the ice-bolt, Rachel
and Kirsty gasped in horror.

"It's Jack Frost!" cried Kirsty.

Rachel looked more closely at the
dancers.

"The dancers all have enormous feet!"
she exclaimed. "And I can see a hint of
green skin through their tights. Oh Kirsty,
they're goblins!"

Cackling with laughter, Jack Frost
created a flurry of ice-bolts, and each
of the goblin dancers jumped onto one
of them. Jack Frost
stood on his ice-
bolt as if it were
a skateboard,
the True Love
Crown dangling
from his arm.

"Those pesky fairies will never get their silly crown back!" he gloated. "And you can't do anything to stop me!"

As he darted away into the sky followed by his goblins, the picture faded and Rachel and Kirsty turned to look at Kate.

"This is terrible!" said Rachel. "We have to get the True Love Crown back!"

"We'll do everything we can to help," Kirsty added.

Kate and the girls visited the gleaming Spiral Tower to see where the True Love Crown belonged, and they said hello to Stanley and Bertram. Stanley told them that Jack Frost had flown away in the direction of his Ice Castle.

"We must follow him there!" said Kirsty in a determined voice. Kirsty and Rachel had visited the Ice Castle before and knew it was a dark, cold and scary place!

Kate nodded. "Let's go back to the palace," she said. "I must tell the queen what we are planning to do."

The girls said goodbye to Stanley and followed Kate back to the palace. Fairies were flitting in all directions, each with an important job to do for the wedding.

"Why don't you wait in the entrance
hall while I visit the queen?" Kate asked.

Rachel and Kirsty agreed at once,
happy to watch all the preparations. As
they approached the palace they saw
Cherry the Cake Fairy fluttering towards
the palace kitchens with the ingredients
for a magnificent cake. In the library,
the Petal Fairies had
spread out a carpet
of bright blooms
and were creating
a wonderful
bouquet. Goldie
the Sunshine Fairy
perched at a glossy
mahogany desk, composing
a spell to ensure that the sun would shine
on the bride and groom all day long.

As the girls reached the entrance hall, they heard the faint strains of beautiful music.

"That must be the Music Fairies practising the *Wedding March*," said Kirsty.

"I've never known the palace to be so full of fairies," Rachel said. "But they all look very solemn. On a day like this, they should be full of happiness and excitement."

"They must be so worried that without the crown there'll be no 'happy ever after' for Princess Grace and her new husband," Kirsty frowned.

"Then we just have to get the True Love Crown back in time," said Rachel. "I want to see our fairy friends looking happy again!

35

An Icy Coronation

Rachel, Kirsty and Kate flew as fast as they could to the Ice Castle. They passed over the green, lush fields of Fairyland to the stark, icy landscape of Jack Frost's realm. When they saw the Ice Castle looming ahead of them, they flew even faster. There was no time to lose!

They zoomed around the castle wall,
keeping a look out for goblin guards.
They had only gone about halfway
round when Kate stopped beside a tall
window.

"Listen!" she said in a whisper. "I can
hear Jack Frost!"

"That's the throne room," said Kirsty,
drawing nearer. "And look – the window
is open!"

They slipped into the throne room and
hid behind the frayed old curtains that
hung in the window. Jack Frost was sitting
on his throne, bellowing at a gaggle of
goblin servants. In front of him, a plump
little goblin was holding up a grey, well-
worn cushion as high as he could. And
on the cushion was the magnificent True
Love Crown.

"There it is!" exclaimed Rachel.

"We must get it back," Kate whispered. "Princess Grace's happiness depends on us."

The plump goblin must have been holding up the crown for a long time, because his arms were starting to droop.

"Don't drop my beautiful sparkly crown!" Jack Frost bawled into his face. "It's going to make me look even more handsome than I already am!"

He grabbed the crown and settled back into his throne with a smug sneer.

"Sneaking into the palace grounds yesterday was one of my most brilliant plans ever," he boasted.

"I knew those soppy fairies would be too busy preparing for the mushy wedding to notice me, and I could find some mischief to do. And then that silly frog guard delivered the crown right into my hands. Ha! Ha! Ha!"

"But what if the king and queen come looking for it?" asked the plump goblin.

"Don't question me!" screeched Jack Frost. "They already have a crown each – they don't need this one. They probably haven't even noticed that it's missing!"

Just then, three goblins dashed up to the throne carrying a large piece of cloth. It looked like a hundred-year-old tablecloth that had never been washed.

"Your cloak is ready," they said in unison.

"About time!" exclaimed Jack Frost, leaping off his throne and snatching the cloak from them. As he placed it around his shoulders, the girls saw that it was made from old bits of cloth, dirty dusters,

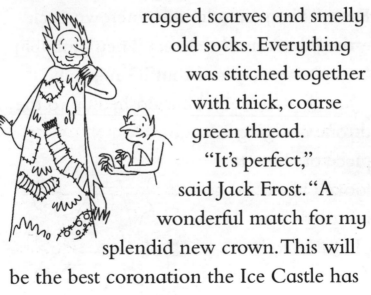 ragged scarves and smelly old socks. Everything was stitched together with thick, coarse green thread.

"It's perfect," said Jack Frost. "A wonderful match for my splendid new crown. This will be the best coronation the Ice Castle has ever seen!"

Kate gave a groan.

"What's wrong?" asked Kirsty.

"A coronation is a royal ceremony that makes someone a king or queen," Kate said in a whisper. "The True Love Crown's magic is activated by royal ceremonies. Even though this won't be a real coronation, the power of the True Love Crown means that Jack Frost will fall in love with the first person he sees after he puts on the crown!"

Kirsty and Rachel gasped as Jack grabbed a hook-nosed goblin servant by the shoulder.

"For a proper coronation, I need an official companion," he said.

"But I don't want . . ." began the goblin.

"Shut up!" bellowed Jack Frost rudely. "You'll do as you're told! Join the procession to the crypt!"

43

Everyone lined up behind a tall goblin
in a pointy ceremonial hat, which kept
slipping down over his eyes.

Jack Frost walked beside
his companion goblin,
holding him in an icy
grip. The other goblins
followed behind, with
the plump little goblin
at the back with the
True Love Crown. Kate
and the girls flitted after
them, staying out of sight.

The procession wound down crumbling
old steps to the crypt. It was very cold
and damp, and ghostly white mould was
growing up the walls. A greenish light
came from glowing stalactites that hung
from the ceiling.

The tall goblin pushed up his hat, trying to balance the edge of it on his eyebrows. He stood on a raised block of slimy stone and faced his master and the gathering goblins. The hook-nosed goblin was still protesting.

"We are gathered here today to witness the coronation of our ... er ..." began the tall goblin.

"... stupendously handsome master," put in Jack Frost through gritted teeth.

"... stupendously handsome master," repeated the goblin as his hat fell over his

eyes again.

"This might be our best chance to take back the crown," Kate whispered.

"It's risky – we're bound to be seen," said Kirsty.

"Then we'll just have to be quick enough to take it before they can catch us," said Rachel. "Come on!"

All eyes were on Jack Frost and the sulky companion goblin. Kate, Rachel and Kirsty swooped down towards the True Love Crown. But just as they reached it, the companion goblin wriggled free from his master's grasp, and Jack Frost had to turn to catch him. He saw the girls and gave a yell of rage.

"Pesky fairies!" he shouted.

He raised his wand and blasted Kate's wand from her hand. Then he hissed a spell, and the glowing stalactites grew downwards from the ceiling as fast as lightning, curving and freezing into an icy cage around the three fairies. They were trapped!

Jack Frost in Love

Kirsty, Rachel and Kate could do nothing but watch the silly ceremony unfold. First, the tall goblin unfurled a scroll of paper and began to read aloud in a high-pitched, singsong voice.

"Do you, Jack Frost, being of cruel mind and spiky body, promise to rule your goblins with unfair treatment and general meanness?"

"I do," said Jack Frost solemnly.

The tall goblin pushed his hat up so hard that it fell off and he had to scrabble around to find it in the gloom.

"Get on with it!" Jack Frost snarled.

The goblin found his hat, put it on back to front, and squinted at the scroll again.

"Do you vow to cause trouble and mischief wherever possible, especially to pesky fairies?"

"I do," said Jack Frost.

"Will he fall in love with the first person he sees for ever?" whispered Rachel.

"No," Kate told her. "Because the coronation isn't a real ceremony, the True Love Crown's magic will only work while Jack Frost is actually wearing the crown. The trouble is, as soon as he puts it on, he will never want to take it off!"

The girls racked their brains to think of a way to escape, but they were well and truly trapped by the stalactites.

The plump goblin clambered onto the shoulders of another goblin and held the crown above Jack Frost's head.

"Jack Frost has vowed to carry out his duties," announced the tall goblin. "I therefore pronounce him Master of the Goblins and ruler of all icy kingdoms!"

The girls held their breath as the True Love Crown was lowered onto Jack Frost's spiky head. As it touched him, he was glaring at his companion goblin. There was a faint glow around the True Love Crown, and then the girls saw his nasty expression change. His tight grip on the goblin's shoulder released, and he stroked his bald green head lovingly. His eyes sparkled and a soppy smile spread across his face.

"Oh, glorious goblin!" he declared, his voice dripping with honey. "Was there ever a goblin more beautiful than you?"

Jack Frost fell to his knees, dropped his wand and clasped both the bewildered goblin's hands in his.

"Your exquisite blotchy green skin fills me with joy," he burbled. "I want to write poems about your perfect hooked nose and adorable huge feet."

The other goblins were all staring open-mouthed. They could hardly believe their ears!

"Stop it!" wailed the confused companion goblin. "I don't like it! I'm scared!"

He struggled to free his hands.

"Give me a cuddle!" pleaded Jack Frost, drawing the goblin towards him.

"NOOOO!" squawked the goblin, trying to get away.

As Jack Frost and the goblin wrestled with each other the crown toppled from Jack Frost's head onto the stony ground and the enchantment was broken. With a wail of horror and anger, Jack Frost flung the companion goblin into the crowd and turned to glare up at his three captives.

"It's a nasty fairy trick!" he bellowed. "That crown is cursed!"

"No it isn't," said Rachel. "It's the True Love Crown – it was just doing its job."

Jack Frost grabbed the crown from where it had landed.

"That's the most disgustingly romantic, mushy, soppy thing I've ever heard in my life!" he screeched.

He hurled the True Love Crown at them with all his might. The girls gasped as it spun through the air and crashed into their stalactite prison, smashing it to icy smithereens.

Kate grabbed the True Love Crown as it fell and it immediately returned to fairy-size.

"Stop them!" Jack Frost screamed at his goblin servants.

But Kate had already zoomed into the corner where her wand had landed, and before the goblins could move, she had used her fairy magic to whisk herself, Rachel and Kirsty straight back to the Fairyland Palace!

Kate, Rachel and Kirsty arrived outside the palace and saw Princess Grace with Mia, waiting for her coach to take them to the palace chapel. They were just in time! Suddenly there was a whinnying sound, and around the corner of the palace trotted four white unicorns with golden manes, led by Leona the Unicorn

Fairy. They were drawing a magical coach made of sparkling glass and trimmed with gold.

As Princess Grace and Mia the Bridesmaid Fairy climbed into the coach, Kate led Rachel and Kirsty to the palace chapel. It was a beautiful building, with an archway of white roses for a door.

Through the doorway, Rachel and Kirsty could see lots of fairies sitting on tiny white chairs, talking quietly and looking very excited.

The Petal Fairies were there, looking after the beautiful flowered garlands that hung from the walls.

"Did you find the crown?" Ella the Rose Fairy asked eagerly.

"Yes," said Kate, "it's back where it belongs!"

"I'll go and tell the king and queen at once," said Ella happily.

She hurried away. Kate waved her wand over the girls, and their everyday clothes were transformed into flowery silk dresses that swirled as they moved.

"They're beautiful!" Rachel said in delight.

"Thank you!" said Kirsty.

Kate led them up the aisle to the front row, where they stood beside the queen, who was about to take her seat. She smiled gratefully at them.

"Once again you have proved yourselves to be our great friends," she said. "Fairyland will never forget what you have done today."

Suddenly there was a commotion at the back of the chapel and all heads turned. A gasp rippled among the fairies. Jack Frost and his goblins had walked in!

The Royal Wedding

"Don't worry," said the queen with a wise smile. "Jack Frost and his goblins were invited to the wedding."

Rachel and Kirsty settled in the front row as Jack Frost strode up and sat beside them. He was still looking very grumpy.

"Lovey-dovey nonsense," the girls heard him muttering under his breath. "The silly princess is welcome to the silly crown. I'd rather live unhappily ever after!"

Just then, the Music Fairies begin to play the *Wedding March*. Everyone stood up as the beautiful bride walked up the aisle with her bridesmaid. She looked radiantly happy, and the prince's eyes sparkled with love as he looked at her.

Jack Frost got up in disgust and stomped to the back of the hall.

Kate placed the True Love Crown on the bride's head, then the king performed the ceremony. As the happy couple said their vows, a glimmering ribbon of fairy dust flowed from the crown and encircled them. The magic was working!

As the king pronounced them husband and wife, the bells began to peal, and the chapel rang with fairy cheers!

Hannah the Happy Ever After Fairy flitted among the fairies, handing out magical, sparkling confetti to throw over the happy couple. The Rainbow Fairies' special wedding rainbow arched over the bride and groom, and joyful music filled the air.

"Thank you all," said Princess Grace. "Now I would like to invite everyone to the palace ballroom for a grand party!"

There had never been such a wonderful party in the history of Fairyland. Every fairy that Rachel and Kirsty had ever met was there. A spectacular feast was laid out on grand tables, and the goblins eagerly rushed forward to scoff the delicious food. Luckily, thanks to the Party Fairies' magic, each empty plate immediately filled up again with more yummy treats! There were enchanted melodies from the Music Fairies. Cherry the Cake Fairy had created a frosted, layered wedding cake decorated with pink icing and sugared roses.

After the feast there were dazzling
displays from the Dance Fairies and
show-stopping performances from the
Showtime Fairies. Destiny the Pop Star
Fairy sang some of her most popular
songs, and even Jack Frost jumped up for
a dance with his goblins!

Rachel and Kirsty danced the night
away among the fairies, spinning and
twirling in the air.

"I want this night to last for ever!" giggled Rachel as she and her best friend danced with Mia and Kate.

"The bride and groom look so happy," said Kirsty with a smile.

Princess Grace and Prince Arthur were waltzing in the centre of the ballroom, still surrounded by the magical glow from the True Love Crown.

"Their love will last for ever," said Kate with a soft smile.

Just then, the music stopped and Grace the Glitter Fairy rose into the air.

"Would everyone be kind enough to step outside?" she asked in her tinkling voice. "Polly the Party Fun Fairy and I have arranged a little surprise."

Everyone gathered outside the palace under the silvery stars.

67

Then the night sky was lit up by a
magical fireworks display!

"Oooh!" gasped Rachel as puffs of
golden glitter exploded above her.

"Ahhh!" said Kirsty as multi-coloured
rockets zoomed into the sky and bathed
the palace in red, green, blue and yellow.

Each amazing firework was more
dazzling than the last. Finally the names
of Princess Grace and Prince Arthur were
spelled out in red and gold lettering, and
the display ended.

"It's late," sighed Rachel, seeing the pink glow of dawn on the horizon and knowing that their time in Fairyland was coming to an end. "We should be going home."

Kate put her arms around them both and gave them a big hug.

"Thanks to you, the prince and princess are starting their lives together with guaranteed happiness and love,"  she said. "That is the most wonderful gift anyone could give them. Thank you from the bottom of my heart."

"Thank you for letting us help," said Kirsty. "A royal fairy wedding is the best celebration in the world!"

69

The girls held hands and waved
goodbye to the happy wedding party.
Then all their fairy friends waved their
wands together, and streams of glittering
fairy dust surrounded them, shimmering
in all the colours of the rainbow. Dazzled,
Rachel and Kirsty closed their eyes, and
when they opened them again they were
standing by the flowerbeds in Tippington
Park.

"Oh Rachel, no time has passed at all!"
said Kirsty.

As she spoke, Kirsty noticed something
strange. The breeze had died down,

but two red roses were
nodding in their
direction.

"Rachel, look!"
she said.

They bent down, and as they got closer, the petals spread out wide. In the centre of each rose was a tiny pink flower corsage brooch, as pink and delicate as the buttonholes at the wedding. Attached to them was a note in gleaming golden lettering:

These corsages will never fade, and will keep their scent for ever.
With love,
Kate the Royal Wedding Fairy.

Rachel and Kirsty pinned each other's corsages on. The sweet smell of roses wafted up to them, and they smiled at each other.

"What are you thinking about, Kirsty?" asked Rachel.

"I was just remembering what happened when Kate put the True Love Crown on Princess Grace's head," said Kirsty. "I think our adventure was wonderful, but the most wonderful thing of all is knowing that the royal couple will live happily ever after."

"And we helped it to happen," Rachel agreed. "Long live the prince and princess!"

Now it's time for Kirsty and Rachel to help...

Honor the HappyDays Fairy

Here's an exclusive extract...

Princess Rachel and
Princess Kirsty!

"We're here, Kirsty!" Rachel bounced up and down in her seat with excitement as she pointed out of the coach window. "Look, that sign says Golden Palace."

Kirsty beamed at her friend. "I can't believe we get to spend a whole week in a real palace," she sighed happily. "I'm beginning to feel like a princess already!"

There were cheers and whoops as the other children on the coach also spotted the sign. Golden Palace, a large and beautiful stately home, was in the countryside just outside the village of Wetherbury where Kirsty lived. The house was open to the public, but Kirsty had never visited it before. However, during the spring holidays the house was holding a special Kids' Week, and Kirsty had invited Rachel to come to Golden Palace with her.

"I can't wait to see our bedroom," Rachel said eagerly as the coach drove through the tall wrought-iron gates. "Imagine staying in a room that was once used by princes and princesses!"

"And I wonder what activities we're going to be doing this week," Kirsty added. "I hope we get to do lots of princess-type things!"

The coach trundled over a drawbridge and then began to wind its way slowly

through the enormous grounds. Like all
the other children on the coach, Rachel
and Kirsty stared excitedly out of the
window, straining to catch their first
glimpse of Golden Palace. But there were
lots of amazing things on the way to the
house that caught their attention, too.

"Look, a petting zoo!" Kirsty exclaimed
as they drove past a field of tiny Shetland
ponies and little white goats. The girls
could also see another field with horses
and donkeys grazing, and pens of baby
piglets, rabbits and guinea pigs. "Aren't
the Shetland ponies cute?"

"There's a lake just over there," Rachel
pointed out. The lake was surrounded
by beautiful willow trees, and ducks and
swans were gliding across the water. "And
look at that enormous white greenhouse,

Kirsty. I can see lots of orange and lemon trees growing inside it."

"I think it's called an orangery," Kirsty replied. "I've seen one before, when we went to visit another stately home."

The coach passed a croquet field with hoops stuck into the grass, and then a very big, complicated-looking maze made of close-growing green hedges.

"That maze has lots of twists and turns," Rachel whispered to Kirsty. "We might get lost in it and need some fairy magic to find our way out!"

The two girls exchanged a smile. Their friendship with the fairies was a very special secret. "Maybe we'll see some of our fairy friends during our stay here!" Rachel whispered.

Competition!

Kate the Royal Wedding Fairy has created this special word wand just for you! Read the clues and write the answers in the boxes below. The last letter of each word is the start of the next one. When you have all four answers, go online to enter.

1. What kind of event does Kate look after?

2. What is Stanley the frog's job?